Even the Crows
Say Kraków

Also by James Hopkin

Winter Under Water

Even the Crows
Say Kraków

❧

JAMES HOPKIN

PICADOR SHOTS

First published 2008 by Picador
an imprint of Pan Macmillan Ltd
Pan Macmillan, 20 New Wharf Road, London N1 9RR
Basingstoke and Oxford
Associated companies throughout the world
www.panmacmillan.com

ISBN 978-0-330-46082-8

1 3 5 7 9 8 6 4 2

A CIP catalogue record for this book is available from
the British Library.

Printed and bound in the UK by
CPI Mackays, Chatham ME5 8TD

Visit www.picador.com to read more about all our books
and to buy them. You will also find features, author interviews and
news of any author events, and you can sign up for e-newsletters
so that you're always first to hear about our new releases.

For Rosie Wright
1981–2007

Contents

◄❧

'Open up, Floriańska Gate, open up.'

But was there really any need? There hadn't been a gate for years.

Besides, she could go under or over the old stone arch.

'Open up,' she whispered, with a laugh that defied refusal.

And then she flew over the top. Ten minutes previously Alina, Alinka (that's little Alina) had descended from low cloud over the Wawel Cathedral. Then she'd seen the sloping tin roofs of the church, bright with rain like a well-scrubbed kitchen table. Already she was wondering: should I land? Then she'd glimpsed the turrets and towers, like peeled half-onions, but upside down. Where to land? She banged a leg against some jutting brickwork with a crucifix perched on top. She remembered not to swear. But the shudder went up her spine and along her upper row of teeth. She bit her tongue. She swore. The chair swerved violently and she came face to face with a toothless gargoyle. But she was not scared; it looked like the man next door who came home drunk on a Saturday night. He always drank without his teeth, you see, just to be on the safe side.

And so over the Floriańska Gate she goes and down to street level, where the peasant women stand up to their ankles in the gathering dusk. Each time they pluck a bunch of blooms from their green buckets and shake off the drops of water in front of them, a little more of the night bursts on the pavement and begins to spread about them. Alinka flies on, somehow unseen. A woman? Why, yes, she's thirty years old, but flying like this, she sees herself as Alinka. Perhaps it's safer, this diminutive Alina. Perhaps she's lighter, smaller, a goblin of sorts, tucked in a pocket of her homeland. And who would have thought she could fly?

Not her mother for sure. She'd been a teacher. And they don't teach you things like that, do they? Or her father? Never! He always wanted to feel himself ankle-deep in the soil. Then maybe Alinka herself? They used to say her imagination would get the better of her, though in her dreams she always travelled underground.

An hour earlier, she'd been in the cafe, Jama Michalika, sitting in a mahogany chair the colour of freshly brewed coffee, no, the colour of the River Wisła at night, no, the colour of Marek's eyes, no, don't think of him, Alinka, she told herself. These great wing-backed chairs are surely built for dreamers, she thought, for thinkers, for fairy tales. They are seats for drinking mysterious green liquids that make you see the world through a match's flame, a seat for eating scrambled eggs from a vessel like a soldier's mess tin, scraping the metal into music with a huge fork, a seat from which to smile at the pretty staff in their lace blouses and black skirts tucked like enormous wings, who have trained their feet to be quieter than the whispers of the regulars who have sat so long in the musky corners that the green velvet upholstery seems to have grown over them so you see only the light of their spittle as if they're gargling fragments of mercury, perhaps from sucking too many thermometers – 'Piotr, are you ill?' And the whites of their eyes! As if locked in perpetual astonishment. Oh, how

Alinka didn't want to end up like them. Well, she'd quite like to be astonished, perhaps, but not forever.

But that seat! A throne, almost, but then you might one day be deposed, and this chair was not for deposing. No, it's a wishing-dreaming chair or, even better, a wishful-thinking chair so that she could wishfully think for a moment that she was Alina, Alinka, little Alina growing up in Kraków all over again. But although she did see herself up there as Alinka, she didn't really want any of that all-over-again business, no, not all over again, because it's far too easy to get stuck in a loop and keep going round and round until your teeth fall out, and she wasn't about to become like her father who spent the last hour of every evening harking back to old times when, apparently, you could look out of the window any time of the day or night and everything would be where it should be and everyone knew what it was they had to do and how much they would get for it and so everyone did it and was grateful and equal and fair. After each meal, her father would pat his stomach and say, 'Now I know where my soul is sitting.' Even though Alinka was due to start a new job in Paris in a week's time, she didn't really know where her soul was sitting. Not at all. For it wasn't sitting, was it? Perhaps dashing, sprinting, flying but not sitting, surely? And how on earth was she going to catch up with it, and so begin a lasting correspondence?

And so Alina, Alinka (that's little Alina) was perched in this wishful-thinking chair staring at her coffee in which she had dropped two thick cubes of sugar as if they were the last of her heavier thoughts. Then she listened to the rustle of the waitresses' skirts which they had trained to accompany the whispers of the visitors, and to complement the light fizz of sugar dissolving in a coffee that was strong enough to straighten your spine, at least for an hour or two. And these waitresses, well, they had also trained their faces to be as still as the sketches on the wall, sketches of grinning misfits, clowns, jugglers, painted birds, and monsters anxious with flight. But, of course, you'd be very rude, not to mention way off the mark, to suggest that the faces of the waitresses were in any way so grotesque. And another thing, these sketches were not always still, especially after a shot or two.

For example, Alina remembered when Marek had insisted – often during one of his blue nights when he would drink only blue drinks – that the subjects of the pictures – this joker with wings, for instance – had flown from one frame to another, thus swapping positions with a sketch of quite a happy trumpet-playing pig. But however hard she looked, Alinka could never see these changes. So Marek, in his frustration, would drink more of his blue liquids because Alina couldn't see. Then, of course, Marek saw more of them – a half-cat-half-human, maybe – would spring across the room from frame to frame, no doubt trailing a luminous limb, but still Alina couldn't see. So she laughed. She touched Marek's wrist. But his eyes were glazing over. So he drank more of his blue liquids. He saw more leaping figures and fauns. He suffered because Alina could not see. Alina suffered because she could not see. And on and on it went until Marek, his teeth turning blue as steadily as ink through sugar, couldn't see any of the pictures at all, and Alina couldn't at all see Marek.

Now Alina alone in the Jama Michalika was listening to a young man playing a violin in an ill-fitting dinner suit which did in a way give him the appearance of a well-dressed cat. You see, it is candle-lit and gloomy in the Jama Michalika, and with a certain tilt of the head, this big bow tie could look like giant whiskers. The more the feline young man strained inside his uncle's shirt, the more subtle the bad notes became, and the more he looked like one of those grotesque pictures, to the extent that Alinka, not doing at all well in forgetting Marek, thought that the unfortunate fiddler might leap from the stage and appear on a table on the other side of the room, perhaps with a fin or wing or elephant's foot attached to his shimmering frame.

So Alina tried to rattle the cup in her saucer as if coercing the young man into melody. When that failed, she drew the bottom of her cup across the edge of her saucer with a porcelain squeak, catching one or two drops, hoping that these might be the notes that the poor fiddler could not find. But when the young man's bow refused to rendezvous with the right notes and his eyebrows had assumed a curve of mournful surrender, Alina took a final mouthful of her coffee and swallowed it with such a gulp that it surely must have travelled down an unintended pipe. If only I was out of here . . .

And then, moments later, she was rising above the street. Don't ask how, don't be incredulous. Do you really *need* the details? In this chair, almost the colour and size of the chestnut pony she'd seen from the bus that morning, she was looking down on Kraków, her city, her home. As no one in the street would have believed it, no one saw it. Though the guy with the orange pretzel cart did turn an eye, but he was probably just checking that his cap was still on his head or else he had a glass eye in which case it was cleaning itself while rotating. And a woman in a stylish suit cut to catch the autumn light tilted her head in the chair's direction, but she had just come out of the hairdresser's and so she was probably angling her fresh bouffant away from the breeze. After her initial astonishment, Alinka herself adapted with ease, as if settling in a train seat as it was pulling away from the platform on its way to Wrocław where Alinka would no doubt be quizzed by her aunt about her regrettable lack of a husband: 'I mean, Alinka, how difficult can it be? Every monster meets its match.'

But from up there, of course, and when not mollycoddled by a cloud, Alinka thought she'd be able to see people talking off the top of their heads. And she wondered: do words float up not down, or is that just the hot-aired words, and the words of levity and love? And she'd be able to see grandparents sitting on the benches in the square talking about their little ones, while leaves were falling on their wise heads, and if not wise heads – for why equate wisdom with old age, when stupidity endures too? – then almost certainly grey heads, though that as well is not guaranteed. What else could she see or do up there, above her city, the city she was leaving? Alinka had no idea. Perhaps she could help someone find their cat?

And so on she flew, a little guiltily not looking for anything, at first, because she'd always thought that the important things would come looking for her though she was beginning to realise that this wasn't at all the case, and as she was such a long way up no one could see her anyway so perhaps it wasn't a good idea, after all. Thirty, my god, in the clouds, and full of doubts! And besides, such a big chair can be a little lonely. And loneliness is not much fun at any altitude. Flying lower over an orchard, she saw three crows, cloaked like judges, sitting on a branch nearby. They nodded in unison. 'Krak-uuuf,' they said, all together, as their verdict, and then again 'Krak-uuuf'. Then, one at a time, they flew off, their great wings flapping like ceremonial robes. Alinka wondered: do the birds talk of their own city in Paris?

A few minutes later, and Alinka sweeps in low down ulica Szewska, and, unseen, drops a coin in the accordionist's tin. Eyes closed, he nods in gratitude to the clamour of the coin. Down every street a flap of wing like a rug being shook of dust as birds scattered to accommodate Alina. But the accordionist played on. And the man scraping music with a big old saw, well, he played on, dragging his bow across the wobbling blade as if his supper depended on it, and some days it did, and really it wasn't much like music, more of a windy whine, which Alinka thought might be how the old man sounded inside. He didn't see her because he was almost blind with cataracts which sat like milk spots on the seats of his eyes, and no one else saw her because they'd never believe that such a feat is possible.

On she flew, twice round the big yellow cloth hall which seemed even more magnificent the second time round. She'd always thought it looked like a giant Battenburg cake, but from up here, the way the light fell across it and set it in the centre of the square, it appeared more solid and majestic and not at all edible, a great symbol of her city, the city she'd been born in and destined to leave. Destined? Well, yes, in a way. Since childhood, every time Alinka bought a new pair of shoes she'd imagined wearing them in a different city: Berlin, London, Paris. So, you see, you shouldn't underestimate what shoes might tell you of your fate, or even how they may walk you to it. Flying on, Alina, Alinka, that's not so little Alina, thank you very much, humbled the pigeons to make way as she planted the thick legs of the chair in their midst. Then, when they all rose up in alarm, she rose up too, and though everyone nearby did look up at this great flapping exodus, they didn't see her behind the cavalcade of wings.

By now, Alinka was beginning to wonder what the point of it was, this flying around the city where she had lived all her life. Perhaps this wishful-thinking chair was trying to show her what she'd miss when she was in Paris. Whatever the case, it was exhilarating all right. She thought at one point that she might have to keep her heart in her purse for safe keeping because her purse had a good strong clasp, and she'd never lost a single grosz, while her heart was threatening to spill its contents, not all of which she was aware of or yet ready to reveal.

In the square, a horse pulling a carriage must have got wind of her because it snorted and shook a leg in her direction so that one of the tourists taking a photo from the back seat, lost his hat, his poise and then his composure, cursed the horse, the driver, and then this godforsaken town, before whispering to his wife that next year, don't you worry, we'll go back to Prague. And one or two dogs barked and ran round in circles, dragging their owners who might have thought the time had come to get someone else to walk these louts who had become almost human in their loutishness. But still no one saw, pointed, believed. Alinka was pretty much alone. In fact, it must be said that such was the clarity of her solitude that she wondered, for an out-sized moment (yes, it was shaped more like an odd fruit than a section of time), if this was to be her fate: Alina, Alinka, little Alina, forever to fend for herself. Especially as a year previously, she had left Marek, her love of ten years. Yes, she'd left him to his visions, his blue potions, his moods of many colours. But now, she felt . . . what was it? He was the only person in the world who would believe the story of her flying chair.

Next, she flew across the town to her favourite church, the Jesuit Church of St Peter and St Paul. As she came down ulica Grodzka, she once again heard a violin but this time it was a melancholy tune played by a woman in a long flapping black dress who stood by a tree, and this woman from above, and in the gathering darkness, looked like one of the crows who had whispered, 'krak-uuuf', and then again, 'krak-uuuf', so perhaps this crow-woman had stepped down from the tree, divested herself of beak and wing, and taken up the fiddle. The music was rising up the bark and racing along the branches and flying out in all directions. The melody was rushing up the street, making nonsense of the cobbles.

It was catching every pillar and cove as it

travelled from sad to solemn in the developing night. And the tremulous notes seemed to hang in the air, on the points of the church's black iron gates, on telegraph wires, on the toes of Alinka's shoes (and these ones would soon walk her round Paris), as the bow found secret corners and hiding places, where soon the birds would fold in their wings, and where perhaps Marek and Alinka had once shared a fateful first cigarette. But Marek can look after himself now, she thought, while wondering if he could.

But the doleful music did hang in the air and about the ears and catch little Alina right in the head, in the heart, in the everywhere. All that she was and all that she wasn't she could feel at that moment, in the music, and she couldn't help but think: I am only thirty. I have loved, I have left, I am leaving. I'm not ready. I don't know. I'm . . . What?

Below her in the street, a young man stood listening to the violin, resting his head against the wall as if warming his ear on a brick, or perhaps he could hear the violin coming up through the foundations and directly from there into the soul that was standing in his shoes. Without his glasses he was sure those statues outside the church were moving on their pedestals, not dancing as such, but moving a little, perhaps even changing places, this way, then that way. Either way, Alina, Alinka, little Alina was all of a tremble, a delicate soul. For those few minutes she hovered, feeling all that she could without bursting her purse, falling out of her chair, or yelling out inappropriate words, for all words were inappropriate now. She cried a little. A tear fell on the young man's head. He patted his short hair, thought that it was a first drop of rain, and hugged himself closer to the wall.

It was getting dark now, and cold, and Alinka still hadn't flown to Kazimierz, the Jewish district. She'd been thinking of it all along, in the back of her mind, where so much is stored, perhaps waiting for the front of someone else's mind to bring it to fruition. And though her knuckles were slowly turning as blue as Marek's teeth during one of his blue nights, she was determined to fly down to Kazimierz. How much time had she spent there over the years? Well, if you can measure time in walks and in sitting on benches in the courtyard amid the synagogues and cafes as the light dimples the panels of the few cars in the square, then, all in all, quite some time. And so off she flew with a swift turn of the chair in the direction of ulica Józefa, high

above a number thirteen tram that was splash-
ing the streets with a light somewhere between
melon and moon.

When she came to Kazimierz, she felt the
usual calm, not quite a sadness, but something
equally rich and reflective. In the near leafless
trees on the square, she again saw those three
crows intoning 'krak-uuuf' and then once
more 'krak-uuuf', before flying off, this time
their wings unfolding like blankets being
readied for the night. And she saw the small
red bulbs aglow like berries above the entrance
to the Ariel restaurant, and she could smell
coffee and warmth and soup.

Then Alina, Alinka, that's shivering little
Alina, flew into the Remu'h cemetery and
stooped low to pick up a few small stones which
she then placed on the top of a headstone, as is
the tradition, to signify the promise of return.

And she would return one day, wouldn't she? Although she would have liked to stay longer, she was pimpled with cold. She even tried to warm herself on the night lights that sat in red plastic collars around the cemetery, throwing strange shadows here and there, including a trembling one of Alinka and her chair. She laughed at how it looked like a giant crow about to take flight, and she thought: perhaps this is enough now, it would be nice to be back in the warm. So she gave a little croak and was gone.

Apple Vapours

Drops of rain, as thick as the fat from a frying pan, leak through the slat in the roof. An old man swears and reaches up to close the hatch. As he does so, he loses his balance and bumps into a squat woman made of fruit sacks and yellow teeth and the smell of all things past. The woman screws up her face like a used tea bag, and lets out an almighty curse, the force of which, combined with the collision and the vehicle's jerky progress, sends her stumbling backwards, her barely assembled bulk landing on the toes of a teenage girl who cracks her heavily applied foundation with a scowl and a burst of expletives. Soon enough, like a foul-mouthed version of Chinese Whispers, the twenty or so people packed in the aisle of the minibus are each cursing the day they were born.

Szlak is one of the lucky ones. He has a seat. He is almost happy in his anonymity, squeezing his athletic limbs between the window, the rise of a wheel and the beery drunk beside him. Indeed, the bus is full of drunkards and grandmothers and scruffy traders, most of whom are on their way back from the market with any produce that hasn't yet been left to the pigeons and rats living stealthily under the stalls. Szlak watches as men with the skin of over-baked potatoes jostle in tatty leather jackets that they don't so much wear as wrap around their bent and puny frames. Their moustaches, as rough as old fishing-tackle caught in the weeds, sometimes refute the presence of a mouth.

The squat woman is still mumbling obscenities. Or is she incanting her rosaries? Szlak knows it's difficult to tell round here, where a tough life and all of its torments are relieved only by a bottle or a blessing. At the woman's feet, there are two large red and blue chequered bags. One contains two cauliflowers wearing crowns of badly bruised nectarines, plus nuts and onions and knuckles of garlic; the other holds enormous apples. These apples are so ripe they are already making their way towards putrescence, their sweet and sickly aroma merging with the fumes of the asthmatic engine, with the breaths made stale by empty stomachs, with the lifetime of cheap cigarette smoke lining the drunkards' souls.

Szlak is heading out of town. To the country. Or, to be precise, to a hunting lodge in a village at the foot of the mountains. A hunting lodge? He laughs to himself when he thinks of the place in those terms. If it's a hunting lodge then perhaps he's the one being hunted! But no, it's not a hunting lodge, it's a small cottage bequeathed to him by a long-forgotten great-aunt. Alas, she had also long forgotten him, but in the absence of any close family, the great-aunt's last will and testament had demanded a search for claimants however thin their blood-resemblance, however precarious their perch on the family tree. Yes, Mrs Helena had insisted that her beloved home shouldn't be left to the wolves and here she didn't mean the wild dogs from the mountains not too many kilometres away, no, she meant the ditch-sleeping vagabonds who wander through these parts, with bracken grown into their beards, and black slugs for tongues.

In any case, three years after Mrs Helena's unattended demise (even her dog had prede-ceased her, though faithfully leaving its bones by her bed), the legal office had finally caught up with Szlak, not an easy task for he was all over Europe at the time, getting by or getting into trouble, which his big frame seemed to attract however well-meaning his intentions. It's not that he didn't fit in, though his character, like his blue eyes with their huge pupils, could flash between malice and tenderness, rather that he'd always had a tendency to make his mark: some sort of dispute over unpaid wages in Slovakia that he had taken into his own hands, a misunderstanding over a woman in Sweden, sheer drunken boredom in Bavaria, and, worst of all, he had to admit it, being asked to leave the UK after he'd given a kicking to a couple of thugs who'd come over all racist toward him and his black friend, his mate from the building site, in a pub one muggy summer night in London.

After the fight, he'd spent several repentant days in a cell just off Oxford Street with a Lithuanian shoplifter who was pleading not to be sent back to the streets. Eventually, Szlak was called before a judge, but not in a court, no, this was just the two of them and a policeman in a small room with barred windows and piles of paper, and the judge explained – having first expressed his delight that Szlak could speak 'reasonable' English, though Szlak didn't add he could also speak three Slavic languages – that one of these men was still in hospital and might not recover and then he hinted strongly that they may have been criminals, these two men, or were, in any case, without doubt, not honourable citizens, and in these circumstances, as Szlak was not from round here, would he be interested in taking his kick-boxing out of the country, and within the next three days, and then the matter would be closed. If, on the other hand, he did not choose to leave, he could well be charged with manslaughter. Shortly afterwards, the big man was breathing an almost nauseating freedom as he paced along the banks of the Thames en route to the coach station at Victoria. From there he took a bus going back to mainland Europe – east!

And so here he is now, once again in transit, but this time in a tin on wheels crammed with hungry souls, their pockets packed with horse-meat. The vehicle is bouncing about as if its suspension was put in all the wrong places just for fun; likewise, the lethal potholes, which come camouflaged as puddles only to swallow a balding tyre. Vertebrae slide up and down spines like the beads of an abacus or perhaps the Rosary again – sinners ever!

The old woman loses an apple or two. The drunkard next to Szlak drops a coin he can't decide is copper or gold until he gives up with a grumble down his chest where he stores most of his grievances between a pair of burned-out lungs. Then he opens a can concealed in a brown-paper bag save for the eye of the sipping slot. He glances sideways at the big man beside him. The man is wearing only shorts and a T-shirt despite the late summer downpour.

Szlak is not unhappy. This might not be home but nor is it hostility. He understands these people. From their curses to their angry elbows, they are not unlike his own. They will allow him to exist unchallenged so long as he does not speak a different language or step beyond his place. Nor does he look like an outsider. He has a shaven head, like many of the young men here, where a thick neck only reluctantly delivers the contours of a skull. Besides, he has a knack of out-staring the curious. As he does now, occasionally, among this cargo of dirty anoraks and rotten fruit, for there are thick-eared louts and sons-of-louts here, all expletives and provocations, because very little else could come out of their mouths, unless cigarette butts and fruit pips and phlegm.

Defying most laws of physics and all laws of safety, the bus lurches on, past village name-signs stuffed with consonants (like a flower-bed taken over by cabbages). Other signs mark the end of each settlement with a red line through a silhouette of a church, a farm, a hut. Szlak smiles to himself because he always thinks this sign should offer instead a silhouette of a bottle, a packet of cigarettes, a confession booth.

Dozens of *babciu*-grandmothers sit on their wooden verandas, many of them shelling peas over a wicker basket, and to the rhythm of the rain on the roof, all of them in flowery skirts, headscarves, and ankle-length black boots that all but double their weight. Piles of chopped logs, their ends the colour of freshly baked biscuits, stand beneath wooden roofs for the winter in the wings. Dogs prowl the length of rope from their kennels, not in fear of intruders but of their possible release. On dirt-track driveways, there are rusting bodies of unrecognizable vehicles, plus early tractors, and a whole series of outhouses looking as though they might not withstand a heavier downpour.

With a large hand, Szlak wipes the window of condensation. He is looking for a particular roadside shrine. Some of these shrines boast figurines of saints on top of a thin column, others

mark a fatal road accident with dead flowers
and a simple wooden crucifix. The shrine he is
looking for has a half-metre-tall Virgin Mary
standing in front of a miniature chapel. Just
beyond this point, and set back thirty metres
from the road, lies Mrs Helena's hut.

The road dwindles into a darkness of trees.
Now that the drunkard beside him has packed
up what's left of his wits and disappeared into
the country dusk, Szlak can lean across the
aisle to peer through the driver's windscreen.
But he can't tell if it's the mountains or more
dark clouds looming ahead. Nor can he judge
the distance. Both time and space are meas-
ured differently out here, he knows. Further
roadside scrutiny yields the candlelit pots of
other makeshift sacred sites. Then suddenly he
spots it, the shrine with the Virgin Mary luminous white against the darkening horizon, her

head bowed in the rain.

Shouting for the driver to stop, Szlak jumps up and grabs his sports bag from the overhead rack. The bus veers to the right as if an anchor has been thrown out behind. The chassis pitches into a sodden grass verge. Szlak thanks the driver and leaps from the second step, ankle-deep into the watery turf. When the bus pulls away, the wheels spray his bare legs. Szlak waves his fists and shouts a curse or two, laughing like a maniac, jangling the keys in his pocket, the first ever place of his own after a lifetime of barracks and boarding rooms, those London nights in a cell, or shacked up with barmaids and village girls and landladies' daughters right across Europe, and sometimes the local prostitute, so, yes, he's now waving his fists and swearing in glee more than animosity, as if he has at last found, if not home, then at least a place to be.

As he howls one long, final 'Whore!', he is suddenly aware of a presence beside him. Resplendently white in the gloom, the Virgin Mary stands in remembrance, her head lowered in shame.

Perhaps still suffering from an excess of delight, or now from something darker, Szlak falls to his bare knees in the mud. He crosses himself, and for the first time in many years. He gives thanks to God and to Mrs Helena. A few seconds later, when he rises to his feet, he kisses the smooth head of the sculpture. He feels the rain on his neck.

Throwing his bag over his shoulder, he makes his way down the lane that's barely a lane, merely a parting of sweet-smelling conifers and slender pines and masses of dense, dripping shrubbery. He trails a hand along the wire fence all but hidden beneath the thick green leaves so that he will not miss the gate. He was told that the gate would be padlocked. Again he jingles the keys in the pocket of his shorts. But he can't find the opening. Once, twice, three times he paces up and down the lane, increasingly agitated, tearing at leaves and stems, sometimes ripping out handfuls of sopping wet greenery. There is a little blood on his fingers. He kicks out. He kicks until whole sections of the fence are trembling. Droplets of water leap from shivering leaves. A hound nearby begins to bark, viciously, which sets off another and another, until the whole village resonates to a savage growling.

Standing in sodden shorts and T-shirt and trainers, Szlak is struck by a slow panic of sweat and tightening muscles, fearful of being denied. As usual, his otherwise gentle temperament is soon discarded when threatened with uncertainty. He swears to himself that he'll find every mongrel barking at him, then he'll twist their necks until they snap. He lets out a howl of his own. Then, angling his body with the ease and agility of someone who knows how it's done, he delivers another violent kick.

This time he is in luck. His foot lands in the right place; the gate shudders open a few inches. There is no sign of a padlock. With an angry push, Szlak forces the gate the rest of the way and strides in, booting aside fir-cones, like a man keen to take possession of his goods lest they quickly turn to dream. He finds himself at the end of a narrow garden. He can't yet see the hut. The grass is tall and thin, trampled by the rain and giving off an earthly smell. The dogs continue their malicious welcome. There are voices, too, close by. Following a faint path, Szlak stumbles over piles of bricks, an old tyre, parts of a horse-drawn plough. The rain is abating but the darkness has swiftly closed in, as it can only do in the country, and beneath the mountains, as if the whole day has, with one sudden gesture, surrendered.

Straining his big blue eyes, Szlak can just about make out the shape of the hut. Key in hand, he marches towards it as best as he can through the wet grass and its hidden obstacles. But just as he is approaching the front door, its tarnished glass and metal design glistening in the rain, he hears voices within. He stops in his tracks. He listens either side of his breathing. Like an animal forced to make a snap decision as to whether it is hunting or being hunted.

Sure enough, there are voices inside. His first reaction is to think he must have the wrong place. But his increased heartbeat urges him to action. He steps forward.

As he fits the key, he peers through the glass. He sees only the bare-brick entrance hall, like a tunnel blown through with neglect, and, further along, the square patch of darkness to the cellar. Alongside this, he makes out the wooden ladder to the attic. He turns the key. And enters.

An upside-down face pops out from the attic. And one the right way up from the hole to the cellar. A smell of smoke and damp earth; shadows drip from the walls. The three heads eye-white each other with alarm.

After a moment, as if to confirm it to himself as well as to the trespassers, Szlak bellows, 'This is my home!' His voice echoes round three derelict rooms. But already the two boys, about fourteen years old, have started to scramble up and down their respective ladders. Yet they haven't bargained on the speed and anger of Szlak. Taking giant strides, he appears at the base of the attic ladder as the first boy slides down, petrified by the sight of this big man blocking out the last of the light. Szlak grabs him and holds him squealing under one arm. Then he pulls up the other from his tremulous perch on the cellar ladder and does the same. He makes them promise to leave him alone. Then he kicks open the rotten back door, carries them out like logs to the chopping block, sets them down in the mud and darkness and whacks them both about the ears. As they scamper off, whimpering, Szlak laughs and cheers, and once again sets the village mutts leaping about at the end of their tethers.

An hour later, Szlak has a candle burning in

two of the three rooms, though you can't really call them rooms, they are more like abandoned caves. The bare brick is cold and blue and crumbling. Loose gravel is strewn across the floor. There's a smell of dogs, of damp, of the whole place being returned to the soil. The only piece of furniture is an old kitchen cupboard which Szlak knows, with a bit of work, he can make good again. Thick cobwebs cover the windows. They undulate like waves in the evening breeze. They are as intricate as the lace the grandmothers take to market.

Mrs Helena's bedroom is saved until the end. Szlak lights another candle. He opens the wooden-panelled door, and is met by a rush of cold, as if the bare walls are made of bones. Szlak feels like he did when he last entered a church, anxious, hopeful, but somehow still a trespasser. In the flickering arc of light he sees two or three simple wooden chairs, a small table, a wedding photograph that has outlived both the frame and its teenage lovers, and a black-and-white portrait of Jesus as a man and a boy from which the embedded jewels have been torn, the holes grown through with moss. High on the wall, and thus well out of the reach of an old woman, and at a strange angle, there's a calendar. The date? 1971. The year of Szlak's birth. Yet he is not stirred by the coincidence. He accepts it as inevitable, as though it is merely further confirmation that this is now his home. He sets the candle down on the table.

Now, immediately in front of him, hanging on the wall, he can make out an embroidered blanket of the style favoured by old women in the country – a display-piece in the summer, a necessity in the winter. Beneath that, on delicate legs, stands a sort of over-stuffed chaise-longue, a distressed divan, its rips exceeding the many patched-up sections. Two filthy pillows lie exhausted at one end.

Szlak gags. For the second time that evening, he falls to his knees. He feels Mrs Helena all about him, her loneliness, her slow and solitary death. Especially after he sees, on the old woman's death-bed, a huge patch of blood as dark as plum jam. He crosses himself and mumbles a half-remembered prayer. He stays there, on his muddy knees on the rough stone floor, in the candlelight, for God knows how long.

Later, having decided that he must, for now, leave Mrs Helena's bedroom as it is, Szlak remembers that he hasn't yet looked at the cellar or the attic. But a candle thrust into the hole in the floor reveals only gravel and rubbish, a small, smouldering pile of which the boys had been trying to set fire to, though without success. Plus a terrible smell of rubble and piss, of abandonment, even death. Like a mine evacuated after a fatal accident.

Next, he tries the attic, first hauling himself up a ladder so thin he wonders if it will support him. He places the candle above and pulls himself up towards the heavens. The air here is different, not at all deathly, even welcoming. He can't believe what he finds. A room just to his liking, lightly furnished in the best country way: elk skins, deer skulls, a recently renovated wood-panelled ceiling, small, carefully crafted wooden crucifixes and animals, a framed picture of a peasant returning from market, another of horses, another of a robin in the snow. Again, he shows no signs of surprise. It does not cross his mind that someone is living here and may soon return. No, he accepts the situation as if it has been arranged expressly for him; after all, hadn't he always believed that one day his luck would turn? He opens his sports bag and takes out the only picture he owns: similar to a Hansel and Gretel scene, a brother and sister hand in hand outside a country hut, though the glass of the frame is cracked. He doesn't know where it came from; he doesn't even like the picture, but he has carried it with him for as long as he can remember. He sets it down on the table beside the narrow bed.

After pulling up the attic ladder that feels as light as balsa, Szlak removes his wet clothes and shoes. Then he wraps his muddy limbs in the warmth of two elk skins. It is not cold outside, just the hinge between late summer and autumn, but it feels good this first fur since early spring, especially after the rain, though he shivers violently when he thinks of Mrs Helena's blanket hanging on the wall below. Staring at the sloping ceiling not far above his nose, he imagines for a moment that he is lying in the hull of a capsized boat. He drifts toward memories of his travels, of a lifetime of camping out, bedding down, stopping over, never, it seemed, on the safe side of things, but these visions are interrupted by the late-night cries of village drunks who squat all night on tree-stumps to gulp from dark bottles of beer or, when times are hard, as they usually are, from small clear flasks of eau de cologne.

After that, and in and out of a deeper sleep, Szlak hears a burst of light rain, like stars falling on the roof. Finally, there is silence, layers of silence that you can only get in the country, where each layer lies listening to the next. In this way, every hour passes as if it contains the whole of the night.

At times, Szlak wakes, startled, rearing like a man possessed, with a shout and eyes wide for a familiar sight. He may have dreamed of Mrs Helena, bleeding to death on her divan. Or he may have dreamed of the man he was supposed to have kicked to within an inch of his life. Or of his endless moving on, of the life that has brought him to this solitary cot in an attic in the country. Each time he wakes, he is reassured by the moon and stars of a clearing sky. Together they throw light on the childhood scene propped up on the table by his bed.

Szlak wakes to a glorious late-summer day, to birds, to cockerels, to the excited yapping of dogs. How long since he heard a rooster! From over the mountains come clouds so soft and shapely that he is certain someone in a village the other side of the peaks has spent the last few months making them. He hears the snorting of horses, the lazy buzzing of sated wasps and flies. After years of toiling in the grim districts of Europe, he had forgotten the pleasures of a simple country life.

That moment, Szlak's reverie is violently disturbed by the crashing of stones on the tin roof just above his head. Then comes a splat at the small window at the end of the bed through which he had been watching the early morning sky. From the garden emanates boyish jeering, along with a disturbance of firs and the forcing of the gate.

Szlak jumps up. Completely naked, he throws himself towards the light. He has trouble with the window. He punches it open. Then he smells the sweet stench of the rotten apple now sliding down the pane.